WHITE FEATHER

WHITE FEATHER

CATHERINE & DAVID MacPHAIL

Barrington Stoke

To Mum

First published in 2018 in Great Britain by
Barrington Stoke Ltd
18 Walker Street, Edinburgh, EH3 7LP

www.barringtonstoke.co.uk

Text © 2018 Catherine MacPhail & David MacPhail
Illustrations © 2018 Mary Kate McDevitt

A CIP catalogue record for this book is available
from the British Library upon request

ISBN: 978-1-78112-734-6

Printed in China by Leo

CONTENTS

CHAPTER 1

Coming Home

It was over. After four long years, the war was finally over. Flags were flying. The band was playing. The whole town was celebrating as the soldiers marched past. The boys were coming home from the war.

But not all of them.

Not Charlie.

Tony stood at the back of the crowd, pressed against a wall. He tried his best to keep his tears from falling. He was a man now, almost sixteen. Men didn't cry.

Charlie.

Tony's big brother, his best pal, wouldn't be coming back. Charlie was lying somewhere in France, in a field of blood and mud. Lost for ever.

I shouldn't have come to the march, Tony thought. *I should have stayed at home with Mother.*

Tony's mother refused to believe her eldest son would never return. It was all a mistake, she said. Charlie wasn't dead. He had come home, she insisted. He was already home. She'd seen him with her own eyes.

Tony would never forget that day. His mother had been waiting for him at the front door when he'd come home from work. "Charlie's back," she'd said, and she'd dragged Tony into the kitchen.

There was no one there.

"Charlie was sitting right here a minute ago," Tony's mother said.

She ran her hands along the back of the wooden chair by the fire, as if she could feel Charlie there still. "I didn't even hear him come in," she told Tony as her face glowed with the joy of it. "I came in the back door with the washing off the line, and there he was, sitting there, so handsome in his uniform. My boy."

And all that day she'd waited for him to come back again, to sit in the chair by the fire, and she'd waited every day since. She never gave up hope.

Even when the news came, Tony's mother refused to believe it. She insisted it was a mistake, that the Army had confused her son with another woman's boy.

Tony hadn't just lost his brother. He had lost his mother too.

The boom of the big drums passing close by jolted Tony out of his dark memories. The crowd cheered.

I should have been with him, Tony thought. *It would never have happened if I had been there, with my brother.* Tony was a year younger than Charlie, but they'd always looked out for each other. Tony would have protected him. He would have found a way to save Charlie.

Yet he knew in his heart there was no point going over it. Nothing Tony could do would change anything. The cheers rose again, and Tony's heart bled with sadness. He wished so much he hadn't come. There was no place for him here.

He'd go now, before anyone in the crowd recognised him. He would slip into the shadows and head home. But as he moved, Tony saw a woman approaching him. Wasn't it Mrs Aubrey, Charlie's old teacher? At first he thought she was going to brush past him without a word. Her eyes never met his. But as she came close she reached out and pushed something into Tony's hand. Only then did she glance at him, with a look that was as cold and hard as the iceberg that sank the *Titanic*.

Tony knew even before he opened his hand what Mrs Aubrey had given him.

A white feather.

CHAPTER 2

White Feather

A white feather, there in Tony's palm. The symbol of cowardice. But Mrs Aubrey wasn't calling Tony a coward. The feather was for his brother.

Charlie had died out there in France, but he hadn't died a hero. He had died a coward. He had died running away from battle, turning his back on his comrades, leaving them to be murdered.

Tony closed his eyes and saw Charlie now. He imagined Charlie standing in front of a firing squad, a blindfold round his eyes. Tony stumbled against a wall – he couldn't get the picture out of his head, couldn't stop hearing the sound of the rifles as they fired at his brother.

No!

Tony put his hands over his ears to blot out the gunfire, but it was inside his head, inside his mind, all the time.

He couldn't understand it. How could his brother be a coward? Charlie was only sixteen when he signed up for the Army. He'd pretended he was older so he could serve his country. A coward wouldn't do that. And Charlie had never run from anything. So what had made him run out there on the battlefield? Tony couldn't imagine it, but everyone said this war was like nothing that had happened before. It was hell – a living nightmare.

When they'd got the news about Charlie, Tony and his mother had been shunned. Neighbours, friends and family turned against them. People who had been friends with them for years spat at them in the street or ignored them as if they were invisible. Not everyone – there were some people who understood, or tried to, but they were few.

In some ways, Tony was glad his mother refused to believe Charlie was dead. That way she didn't have to imagine her son being dragged to the firing squad, screaming in terror. Or tied to a chair and carried to his death.

"Not my Charlie," their mother had yelled when the news came. "Not my Charlie."

And then she had sunk back into her dream that he would return, that he would be back to sit in the chair by the fire. She waited for her son to come home.

Tony was grateful that he met no one on his way back home from the march. His mother was sitting in her chair by the fire. She glanced up at Tony, smiled and asked, "Did you have a nice time, son?"

Tony felt the feather still clutched in his hand. He slid it into his pocket and said, "It was fine."

His mother nodded and went back to staring into space.

Tony looked at Charlie's photo on the mantelpiece. It had been taken when Charlie joined the Army. He looked like a boy, just a boy – too young to be in uniform. He was holding his rifle and smiling at the camera.

Charlie, Charlie, what did you do? Tony thought, trying to send his questions from this world to the next, hoping that they might reach his brother and he'd get an answer. *What happened out there? You were all alone, and I should have been with you.*

Now Tony couldn't keep the tears from flowing. His brother had died, alone and afraid, thought of as a coward. And as all Charlie's comrades had been killed, there had been no one to speak in his favour.

So Charlie had been shot at dawn.

CHAPTER 3
The Visit

A few days after the march, a young man came to the door. More a boy, in fact – he couldn't have been much older than Tony. He had a ginger tuft of hair and freckles, making him look even younger, and he was still in his uniform. Tucked under his arm was a brown paper parcel tied up with string.

When Tony opened the door, the boy's eyes widened and he stepped back.

"You gave me the fright of my life there, pal," the boy said, and blew out his cheeks.

"Thought I was seeing a ghost. You're Charlie's spitting image."

"I'm his brother, Tony," Tony explained. He paused a moment, then spoke again. "You knew Charlie?"

The boy nodded. "Just for a while. My name's Harry Tait. Charlie was a friend – that's why I'm here." Harry took the parcel from under his arm and handed it to Tony. "I offered to take his things back."

Tony didn't know what to say – Charlie's things, his life and his death, wrapped in brown wrinkled paper. He stared down at the package, then back at Harry.

"Was it bad out there?" Tony asked. It was a stupid question, but the first thing he thought of.

"You've got no idea," Harry said. "Mud up to our knees, cold all the time. Friends dying every day ..." His voice broke, then he added, "I'm that glad I'm home." He shook his head. "I'm so sorry, I shouldn't have said that. At least I'm getting home."

"Did you see Charlie at the end?" Tony asked.

"Not after he was arrested. But don't think bad of him, Tony. Charlie was just scared – we were all scared – and he ran. My guess is that he didn't even know what he was doing. There were times I would have run – I don't know what stopped me."

Tony said softly, "Maybe you're not a coward."

Harry shook his head. "Your brother wasn't a coward, Tony. Charlie refused a blindfold right there in front of the firing squad – did you know that? Would a coward have done that?"

Charlie had refused a blindfold? *Harry was right*, Tony thought, *a coward wouldn't have done that*.

Tony didn't want Harry to go after that. He had to hear more about his brother. "Can you come in for a bit?" Tony asked. "Have a cup of tea maybe?"

Harry stepped inside the house. Tony could see he didn't want to. He was glad his mum was lying down in the other room. Tony wanted to talk to Harry – he wanted to know about Charlie's life in the trenches – but he didn't want his mother to hear what Harry had to say.

Tony ushered Harry to a seat at the table. His ma always kept a kettle heating on the black grate of the fire. Tony lifted the kettle and filled the teapot.

Harry laughed. "My ma does that too. Always keeps a kettle on the boil." He put on a croaky old lady's voice and said, "Just in case anybody needs a cup of tea."

That made Tony laugh too. "Mothers," Tony said. "The same the world over."

Tony took a seat across from Harry and slid a mug of tea towards him. "I'm sorry to ask you this, but it's just that we know nothing about what happened. How bad was it?"

Harry curled his hands round the mug, as if to warm them. "Don't know that I can tell you much," Harry said, and shrugged. "Me and Charlie, we were just boys. We didn't know what we were doing. We relied on the Sarge to keep us right. He was a good bloke."

"He didn't make it home?" Tony asked.

Harry shook his head and let out a long sigh.

I shouldn't be asking him to relive this, Tony thought, but he couldn't let Harry stop.

"I remember the first time we went over the top," Harry said. "Me and Charlie together, climbing out of the trenches. We were so scared. Didn't know what we were doing. There was smoke everywhere. We couldn't see nothing. The smoke and the stench of the fumes and ... the smell of death – it made me sick. Then a whistle blew. Charlie shouted out, 'What does that mean?' And another voice shouted back, 'It means we go back. We retreat.'

"We couldn't understand it," Harry continued. "We hadn't done anything. What was the point of it all? The Sarge came running and dragged me and Charlie to our feet. I was shaking and couldn't stop. As the Sarge pulled us back, we could see figures lying on the ground. Our mates, who'd been running with us just minutes ago, were never getting up again. And for what? They died for nothing. No wonder I was shaking."

Tony could see Harry's hands were shaking now too, as he remembered these awful moments. "Maybe you shouldn't go on, Harry," Tony told him. "I'm sorry I brought this all back to you."

But Harry didn't answer. He just carried on, as if he was still there in the trenches, bringing the scenes alive for Tony.

"It was horrible. It was a mess. But the worst thing was that nobody seemed to know what was going on – even the officers, even the Sarge, and we thought he knew everything. Our world was all darkness and smoke and deadly gunfire. It was like living in hell. Nothing grew there. The trees were all stunted, the mud was up to our knees."

Harry stopped for a moment, looked at Tony and said, "And do you know what Charlie used to say? He'd say, 'Maybe we've already been killed, Harry. Maybe we're already dead.' Your brother said some funny things. But I wondered if he was right. We were dead and this was hell." Harry took a long drink of his tea, then added, "I liked Charlie. Your brother was always there for me. I just wish I could have been there for him at the end. But we got split up in that final push."

"Charlie was always there for me too," Tony said. "He was always the brave one of us. I don't understand why he ran away ... Maybe it was a mistake, Harry."

But Harry shook his head. "One of the officers saw Charlie running, Tony. Lieutenant Fortune saw him. I hate to say it, and I'm not blaming Charlie, but you can't get away from the fact that he was deserting his post."

CHAPTER 4
The Letter

After Harry left, Tony checked his mother was still sleeping. She slept so much nowadays. Tony guessed that by sleeping she could escape the truth for a while and dream that her son would come home.

He left her sleeping in the wall bed in the kitchen and closed the door softly so she wouldn't hear him opening the parcel. Tony didn't want his mother to see Charlie's things. It would be too much for her. It was almost too much for him. He used his penknife to cut the string, and the brown paper fell open. Inside, there wasn't much. A khaki shirt, a pair of trousers, a long coat the same colour as the shirt, Charlie's tobacco tin. All that was left of his brother. Tony lifted the shirt and held it to his face. He was hoping the scent of his brother might still linger there.

Something crackled in the shirt pocket. Tony slipped his hand inside and pulled out an envelope.

On the front, in Charlie's scrawling handwriting, were the words: *To Tony and Ma.*

There was one sheet of paper inside the envelope. It had ripped edges, as if it had been torn from an old notebook.

A letter from Tony's brother.

He should have known Charlie would send him a letter. He'd sent letters before. But this was different. This letter was Charlie's last. The last words he had written before he died.

CATHERINE & DAVID MacPHAIL

Tony couldn't bear to read it, yet he knew he must.

The paper shook in Tony's trembling hand. His brother's final message to his family. The handwriting was scratchy, and Tony could picture Charlie at a table, bent over the page, biting his bottom lip – the way Charlie always did when he was thinking hard. The image was so clear in Tony's mind it felt real. It felt as if Tony was actually watching it in one of those new moving pictures.

Dear Ma and Tony,

> *Fortune has deserted me. They*
> *have taken me to prison. Heaven*
> *Knows why. I have done nothing*
> *wrong. I only told the*
> *Truth. Don't worry. I will*
> *Make sure I do my best to get out of it.*
> *Trust in God as I trust in*

Him. I hope you understand, Tony.
Tell Ma I love her.
> *Remember the games we played as boys, Tony? Remember now.*

Your loving brother and son,
Charlie.

Tony's tears fell on the page. His brother had written this after he'd been arrested, after he'd been sentenced to death. Charlie had done nothing wrong. Of course he hadn't. It wasn't fair. He had refused a blindfold. A coward didn't do that.

I will make sure I do my best to get out of it.

But Charlie hadn't got out of it. He was dead, and another vivid image of Charlie being dragged in front of the firing squad flashed into Tony's mind.

No! Not dragged. Tony saw a new vision – his brother walking to his death, proud and tall, refusing to be afraid.

Remember the games we played as boys.

How could Tony ever forget? What great fun they'd had, what adventures.

I hope you understand.

Understand what?

Tony sat back in the chair, the letter still clutched in his fingers. There was something funny about this letter. And the more he thought about it, the stranger it seemed.

Fortune has deserted me.

His brother, normally so matter-of-fact, would never have used such a word as "fortune". Charlie would have written "luck". Luck has deserted me.

Fortune.

Tony had heard that word before, from Harry Tait. What was it? It only took a moment for him to remember. The name of the officer who saw Charlie running away. Lieutenant Fortune.

Tony read the letter again. It was written in a strange way. Long lines, short lines, not like a normal letter at all. Like it was hiding something else. Tony read it again. Why did Charlie mention the games they used to play?

Secret codes! It suddenly came to Tony. They'd often played spies or detectives together as children, which meant making up secret codes that no one else understood.

Was this what Charlie had meant? Tony tried to remember some of the codes they had used. But there had been so many. Tony guessed Charlie would have made it an easy code, not a difficult one – after all, this was the last letter Charlie had written, on the day of his death.

Tony looked again at the letter.

Fortune was the first word, as if it was important he read that first. Tony remembered the first-word code, where the first word of each line would make up the message. Could it be that simple? He read the letter again.

> *Fortune has deserted me. They*
> *have taken me to prison. Heaven*
> *Knows why. I have done nothing*
> *wrong. I only told the*
> *Truth. Don't worry. I will*
> *Make sure I do my best to get out of it.*
> *Trust in God as I trust in*
> *Him. I hope you understand, Tony.*
> *Tell Ma I love her.*

That was it. That was Charlie's message:

Fortune knows truth. Make him tell.

So Charlie wanted Tony to help, to find out the truth.

"But how do I do that, Charlie?" Tony whispered the words as if his brother was there in the room with him, as if he could answer.

For a second Tony was sure he heard his brother's familiar voice in his ear, saying, "Fortune knows the truth, Tony. Make him tell."

And Tony answered, "I'll do my best, Charlie."

But how on earth was he ever going to do that? How was he ever going to find out what really happened to his brother?

CHAPTER 5

Finding Fortune

Tony spent a few days trying to work out what he should do. He had to find this Fortune. He had to make him tell. But make Fortune tell *what?* Maybe he had been mistaken and Charlie hadn't been running away? If Fortune had known more about Charlie, if he'd known the kind of boy he was, then he would have realised that.

Fortune knows the truth.

So perhaps Fortune already knows and he's afraid to admit his mistake? Tony wondered.

But *how* could Tony find Fortune? Harry Tait was the only person who might have the answer. Harry had given Tony his address and told him to get in touch if he ever wanted to talk.

So one day after work, Tony made his way to Harry's. He lived in one of the mill workers' cottages on the other side of town. As Tony walked along, he noticed a buzz in their small mill town that hadn't been there for a long time. The streets were busy. Life was getting back to normal after the war – at least it was for most people. Not for Tony.

Harry's house was one in a long line of red-brick cottages. Tony found Harry in his shirt sleeves at the front of the house, working in the small patch of garden. Harry looked surprised to see Tony, but his face fell when Tony told him what he wanted.

"You don't want to do this, Tony," Harry said. "It'll do no good. Put it behind you."

But Tony couldn't do that. He told Harry, "I can't – I have to find Fortune. I just want to ask him what really happened that day."

Tony couldn't tell Harry about the letter. He couldn't tell him about Charlie's secret message. Harry would think he was being daft, grasping at straws, so Tony wouldn't have to accept his brother was a coward.

"And what good would that do, Tony?" Harry said. "It'll just hurt you more. And do you think Fortune's going to talk to the likes of you?"

"I'm going to try, Harry," Tony told him. Nothing was going to make him change his mind. "Do you know where Fortune lives?"

"Of course I know. Fortune boasted about it – always goin' on about his family, his estate, his great uncle who fought at Waterloo. Ha!" Harry laughed. "My grandfather fought at Waterloo as well – the station, that is – after he got thrown off a train!"

Tony didn't laugh back but asked, "Do you think I could get a job at Fortune's estate, Harry?"

"I'm telling you, it's best keeping back from the likes of him, Tony," Harry warned. "Your brother wouldn't want that."

But Tony knew that was exactly what his brother wanted.

"But you'll get work there all right," Harry said reluctantly, when he couldn't persuade Tony not to go. "With so many men not coming back from the war, they'll be desperate for workers."

Tony thanked Harry, but he didn't look happy, and only tried to stop Tony again. "You could get into a lot of trouble," Harry told him. "And your ma has already lost one son – you don't want to bring her more pain."

Tony knew that was true, but he had no choice. "I have to do this for my brother, Harry."

*

It wasn't easy getting someone to look after Ma. Tony couldn't leave her on her own, not now. But his aunt Ellen came to the rescue. She said she'd be happy to come and stay with Ma when Tony told her he'd found a better-paying job, away from home. Of course it was a lie that he already had the job. When had he learned to become such a liar?

Leaving Ma was difficult. She clasped Tony's hand and wouldn't let go.

"Don't you leave me," she begged him. She was so afraid of losing another son.

Tony hugged his ma and told her over and over, "I'll be back – I'm only going for a new job. But I'll be back."

All the time he was thinking, *Am I doing the right thing?*

But Charlie was relying on Tony, and that was his answer. It was as if his brother was by his side, whispering in his ear, "Fortune knows the truth. Make him tell."

CHAPTER 6
Fortune's Estate

It was a long bus ride to the place where
Fortune lived, on country roads that wound
past farms and villages. Tony was dropped off
beside a post office and had to walk the rest
of the way. It was raining – a hard rain that
bounced off the rooftops, spurted out of gutter
pipes and seeped into Tony's bones. Finally,
Tony came over the brow of a hill and there
it was laid out below him: Fortune's estate, a
great sweep of fields and meadows, dotted with
buildings.

The house was the grandest place Tony
had ever seen. It was surrounded by trees and

a manicured garden that was thick with rose bushes and neatly trimmed hedges. The grey stone building rose up three floors high and was edged with turrets and towers. Tony had lived in a house of just two rooms all his life and had shared a bed with his brother until Charlie had left for the war. Why did Fortune need anything so huge? Because he was an officer and a gentleman?

The sight of the place made Tony angry. Fortune was living in luxury, in a vast house, sleeping every night in a comfortable bed. Meanwhile Charlie slept for eternity in the cold, damp earth of France.

Harry had been right – getting a job was easy. So many men hadn't returned from the war, and the estate needed a boy to help out with odd jobs. Tony was to work on the grounds with Joe the gardener.

Tony watched for Fortune carefully, but it took three days to catch a glimpse of the man. At least, Tony thought it was Fortune – he saw a figure stepping into a black car in the distance. He was tall, slim and wearing a brimmed hat that hid his face.

"Is that Fortune?" Tony asked Joe.

Joe was an old man with a short temper. He looked older than he was. Both of Joe's sons had died in the war at Gallipoli, and he just couldn't get over it. Tony knew it was their deaths that had aged him. Joe snapped out an answer to Tony's question, "It's *Lieutenant* Fortune to you, and he's a war hero. And your boss. Don't you forget it."

"Do you like him?" Tony asked.

"Why do you ask that?" Joe barked.

Tony shrugged. "Just wondered."

"Don't ask any more stupid questions," Joe said.

Tony kept quiet after that but kept watching and looking for a chance with Fortune. The problem was, Tony could never get close to him. After a couple of weeks, Tony began to wonder if he should just quit his job and go home. He was getting nowhere. Maybe he was wasting his time. Then Tony thought about Charlie, and about his final letter, and he knew he couldn't let him down.

At last, Tony's patience was rewarded.

"Windows need washing," Joe told Tony one day, three weeks after he'd arrived. "You're not afraid of heights, I hope."

Tony looked up at the three floors of the big house. Even if he had been scared of heights, he would not have admitted it. Here was his chance. Tony imagined himself climbing into one of the windows and searching room after room. He would find Fortune and confront him at last. "You know the truth about my brother!" Tony would say. "Tell me!"

Joe punched Tony's arm to wake him from his daydream. "You're in a dream, boy," Joe said. "Get a bucket and get up that ladder."

As the sun rose in the sky, Tony washed window after window. But he couldn't get in the house – not one of the windows was unlocked. Tony was up and down the ladder for hours, moving it from window to window, filling his bucket again and again with fresh water. And there was no sign of Fortune in any of the rooms.

It was late afternoon when Tony reached the walled garden at the back of the house. He placed the ladder outside the French windows and climbed to the upper floor. Tony soaked his cloth and slapped it on the glass. The sound

made someone inside the room turn sharply –
Tony hadn't noticed anyone in there before.
But now Tony saw him: Fortune. This close, he
was much younger than Tony had expected,
with dark hair and a thin moustache that Tony
guessed was Fortune's attempt to mask his
youth.

Fortune swung round and stared at Tony.
His body seemed to sag. *What did he see*, Tony
wondered. A face staring at him, the dripping
water on the window distorting the features.
Was that why Fortune looked so afraid? He let
out a low moan and then ran at the window,
screaming like some kind of banshee.

Tony stepped back, but there was nowhere
to step back to. The ladder began to topple.
Tony felt himself falling backwards, and then,
nothing.

CHAPTER 7

We Meet at Last

The room was swimming when Tony opened his eyes. But what room? Tony saw an ornate ceiling, a grand golden fireplace, and shelves and shelves of old dusty books. A face floated into Tony's view – a woman's face. Pretty, but creased with concern. "He's awake!" the woman said, sounding relieved.

Her voice seemed distant. Tony tried to sit up, but the room swirled around him so he lay back again.

"He's a strong lad, Miss Alice," came Joe's voice. "He'll be fine." Then Joe's arm was on Tony's elbow, trying to lift him.

The woman with the pretty face, this Miss Alice, shook her head and said, "No. Leave him for a bit. I have some strong tea coming."

The tea helped. Tony sat up at last and looked around him. Miss Alice's pretty face was framed by dark curls. Joe stood by the French windows, clutching his cap in his hand. And in the corner, almost as if he was hiding there, stood Fortune.

"My brother is so sorry," Miss Alice said. "He didn't mean to scare you." She smiled over at Fortune, but he didn't smile back. He was staring at Tony.

"Weren't Lieutenant Fortune's fault," Joe insisted. He glared at Tony as if he was to blame.

At last Fortune spoke, but he didn't move from his corner. "I … I just didn't expect to see anyone at the window." Fortune fidgeted with the hem of his jacket. His face was white, cold, and there was a sheen of sweat on his forehead. "Not two floors up," Fortune added. He tried a flicker of a smile, but it didn't reach his eyes.

Miss Alice explained, "The war. It has made my brother very nervous."

"I'm not nervous, Alice," Fortune said. He sounded cross, as if he was scolding his sister, but Alice just smiled at him.

"He went through a lot in the war," Miss Alice added. "Everyone did."

But some of them came back, Tony thought. *My brother didn't.* This was Tony's chance to say something to Fortune, but he had such a headache. He could hardly talk. He felt sick.

Joe grunted and said, "We'll get out of your hair now, miss." Joe took Tony's arm. "Come on, lad."

"I hope you're feeling better," Miss Alice said. Fortune said nothing more, but his eyes never left Tony.

Miss Alice came into the garden with Tony and Joe and whispered, "I am sorry. My brother suffers badly with his nerves. You gave him rather a scare."

Tony caught a flash of his own reflection in the window. *That was it*, Tony thought. *My face. Fortune thought I was my brother. He saw a face at the window, its features blurred by the water, and Fortune thought my brother had come back.*

And why would my brother's face scare him so much, thought Tony, *unless he has something to hide?*

CHAPTER 8

An Opportunity

For days afterwards, all Tony could think about was finding a way to talk to Fortune. But it seemed that after the incident at the window, Fortune left the house even less. Joe had told Tony that Fortune took a walk in the gardens every morning before the sun was up, but Tony had never seen him. Tony did see his sister though, Miss Alice, picking flowers in one of the many gardens or going out in the car.

A letter from Tony's aunt arrived one day. He read it while lying in his bunk in the workers' quarters. The rain was back, and it battered at the window and ran down the glass in waves. The letter said that Ma wasn't well. Tony wasn't to worry, Aunt Ellen told him, but every word written in the letter made him worry. His aunt explained that his ma kept seeing Charlie. She was sure he was there in the house with her. Ma's neighbours were getting angry with all her carry-on, shouting and crying in the back yard, calling her son's name. Ma was trying to hold on to a hope – an empty hope – that they would realise the truth. That her son was no coward.

Your ma talks about Charlie all the time, Aunt Ellen wrote, *talks about being with him soon. That's why she keeps seeing him, she says, that he's come for her.* Tony knew his aunt was worried, even if she told him not to be. It made finding out the truth all the more urgent.

Help me, Charlie, Tony thought as he gazed out at the rain. *Help me.*

*

Later that day, Tony was pulling up weeds by the front door of the big house when Miss Alice came out. Tony swiped off his cap and muttered a good morning.

Miss Alice smiled when she saw him and asked, "How are you now, Tony?"

"I'm fine, Miss," Tony answered, when really he was still bruised from the fall.

"Good," Miss Alice said. She looked up at the sky and added, "It's going to be a fine day."

Tony watched her climb into the car, and she even gave him a friendly wave as she drove off. She seemed nice, this Miss Alice – nothing like her arrogant brother. Tony was sure Fortune was hiding something.

With Miss Alice gone, Fortune was alone. There in the house, alone. Tony would never have a better time to confront him. But it was a daring thing for an estate worker to do – to go into the big house without being asked. Yet Tony left his weeding and made his way to the walled garden at the back of the house. Earlier that morning, Tony had noticed that the French windows were open. They still were.

He looked around to make sure Joe wasn't about, but there was no one to be seen. Tony took a deep breath and leaped over the wall, as easy as a monkey. He sprinted across the lawn and stepped into the house.

In spite of the sunshine outside, inside it was dark and cold. Tony stepped softly from one room to another. He listened for another footstep, wary of a maid suddenly appearing. He looked up the wide staircase but knew that if he climbed up there it would seem even stranger if he was found. He heard a door opening on the first floor and caught his breath. It had to be Fortune.

Tony moved silently up the stairs. It reminded him of the games he and Charlie used to play as children. They were soldiers on a secret mission, evading the enemy, and making one sound would cost them their lives. Again he felt that Charlie was beside him, whispering in his ear, "Don't make a sound, little brother."

Tony stood at the door for a moment and heard movement inside. He knew he had to do it now – this was his best chance.

Fortune didn't hear Tony open the door and come into the bedroom. It was only when Tony's feet tapped on the wooden floor that Fortune turned. His face drained of all colour. Tony was sure Fortune was about to faint. He seemed to sway, and he stumbled against the wall. He reached out his hand, as if he could stop Tony moving towards him.

"Stay away from me," Fortune said. He moved to the fireplace. "Get away."

Tony wanted answers. He needed to know the truth about his brother, but the words wouldn't come.

Speak, Tony told himself. *Now is the time.*

The arrogance on Fortune's face was replaced by fear.

He thinks I am *my brother*, Tony thought. *Come on, speak.*

"Tell the truth," Tony blurted out at last. "You know the truth."

Fortune stared back at him, terrified.

"Tell the truth," Tony said again.

Tony was sure he was about to hear what had really happened to his brother. The words hung on Fortune's lips.

CHAPTER 9

He Thinks I'm Charlie

The door of the room flew open. Miss Alice stood there, staring. She looked from Tony to her brother. Fortune had slumped to his knees, looking weak and frail. Miss Alice glared at Tony – all her kindness and gentleness towards him was gone in an instant. She was a tigress defending her cub. "What are you doing here?" she snapped.

Tony didn't answer, and Miss Alice ran to her brother. "What have you done to him?" she demanded.

"Nothing. I just wanted ..." Tony began, but Miss Alice waved his words away.

"You don't understand," she said, "no one does, what my brother has been through in this terrible war."

Tony wanted to shout back at her: *What your brother's been through? At least he came back. My brother didn't.* But then Tony would have to explain why Charlie hadn't returned. He'd have to tell her Charlie had been shot as a coward. Tony didn't want Miss Alice to know that. So he said nothing.

"I'd like you to get out of here," she said. "Now."

Tony had no choice. The butler was by his side, tugging at his arm. "I meant no harm ..." Tony said. "I just wanted ..."

But Miss Alice didn't hear, didn't listen. She was too busy tending to her brother.

I've let you down, Charlie, Tony thought as he was pulled away. *I almost had him, and again I let you down.*

But Tony wouldn't give up. He would find another way.

*

Tony tossed and turned in bed that night. It was no good – he couldn't sleep. All he could see when he closed his eyes was Fortune, with his arrogant face, staring at him, and then that arrogance turning to fear. Tony sat up and caught sight of a face in a dark corner of the room.

It was Charlie's face.

Charlie, in the room with him, begging him to help. After the first jolt of shock to see his brother, Tony wasn't scared. He could never be scared of his brother. "I'm sorry, Charlie," Tony whispered.

It was only then that he realised he was talking to himself – his reflection in the cracked mirror on the wall. Not a ghost at all.

How alike we are, Tony thought. *Me and my brother. We could have been twins. Everyone always said so. Fortune thinks I am my brother. From that first day when he saw me staring at him in the window, water trickling down my face, he thinks I am my brother. And I've scared him.*

Tony had scared Fortune again when he had walked into that room today. He'd scared him so much Tony thought he might be ready to tell the truth.

But what if Tony could go further – what if he could make Fortune believe that he really *was* Charlie, the soldier who had come back to haunt him? What if Fortune thought the soldier who had been shot at dawn had returned from the dead?

It would never work, Tony told himself. *Of course it would never work.* But then he paused – for a moment there, in the cracked mirror, Tony had almost believed *he* had seen Charlie's ghost. So why wouldn't Fortune believe it? The idea grew in his head. How Tony could do it. When he could do it.

By the time dawn broke, Tony had a plan, and nothing was going to stop him.

He was going to become his brother's ghost.

CHAPTER 10

The Haunting

The morning mist lay thick on the ground and draped itself between the branches of the trees like cotton wool. Tony waited between two trees within the walled garden, standing as still as death, almost hidden in the mist. He wore his brother's long great coat from the parcel Harry had given him.

Tony didn't have long to wait. Fortune came out of the French windows of the house and stood on the terrace. Tony could see he was trembling, even from this distance. Fortune's hand shook as he lit a cigarette. Spirals of smoke rose up from it and were swallowed by the mist. Fortune's eyes darted around, and for a moment he didn't see Tony standing there. Not until Tony moved, just a bit, just so he caught Fortune's attention, to make his eyes dart to the figure in the trees. Fortune stumbled and held on to the back of a garden chair to stop himself from falling. He shook his head and spoke.

Tony could not hear him, but he knew what Fortune was saying.

"Leave me be. Leave me be."

Tony emerged from the shadows, veiled in mist. Fortune shook his head as if he could shake the image away. The cigarette dropped from his lips. Tony could almost read Fortune's thoughts: *This isn't real. This can't be real. It's my imagination, it can't be happening.*

Tony took a step forwards and pointed his finger at Fortune. Fortune stepped back and shouted, "Leave me be!"

Tony moved closer. Fortune's cry became a scream of terror: "Leave me be!"

Tony knew Alice would hear that cry. It was time for him to go. Fortune covered his face with his hands, and Tony took the chance to slip over the wall. By the time Alice came running out of the house, he was gone from the garden. But Tony stayed low on the other side of the wall and listened.

"He was there again, Alice," Fortune told his sister.

"No one is there." Alice's voice was a worried whisper, but Tony could still hear her.

"Who do you think you saw?" Alice asked her brother. But Fortune didn't answer, and after a moment Alice tried to tell him again, "There was no one there."

Tony knew it was cruel, what he was doing, but it was for his brother. It was for Charlie. And he was close – Fortune was close to breaking. Tony had to keep it up.

*

Tony returned that night. He stood in the garden between the same trees, just as he had done that morning. He stood there for hours, watching the house. Just before midnight, a curtain on the first floor was pulled back, and Fortune's face appeared.

He peered out as if he hoped he was wrong, as if he hoped that there was no figure there. Tony stood like a dead man, until he raised his hand and pointed right at the window. Fortune stepped back. The curtains dropped shut. Tony knew Fortune would call for his sister now.

Moments later, a ribbon of light beamed across the garden, and Alice looked out from the French windows. But by then, Tony was behind the wall. He didn't move until the beam of light vanished and the garden was dark again.

*

He was back in the garden before dawn the next morning, but today Fortune was too afraid to even step out of the doors. He stood inside the house. Tony could see him. Fortune was trying his best not to look, but it seemed he couldn't stop himself. Once again Tony pointed. He wanted to shout – to call out that he would never give up. But Tony stayed as silent as the grave.

Fortune moved further back into the house and cried out for his sister. "Alice! He's back."

For Tony, there was no time to waste. Alice would be there in minutes, never far from

Fortune's side. Tony climbed over the wall, crawled until he was hidden in the trees and then he ran.

*

Tony was working at the stables when Joe came up to him later that day. "Come on," Joe said. "Miss Alice wants us out in a search party."

"A search party? Searching for what?" Tony asked, as if he didn't know.

Joe shook his head and explained, "That poor young lad's seeing things. It's the war – it did something terrible to him, it did."

Tony's blood chilled. Poor young lad! He refused to feel sorry for Fortune. He wanted to tell Joe just what sort of a man Fortune was. A man who kept the truth hidden. A man who let his brother die.

Joe went on, "Miss Alice thinks someone is after him. Seems the poor lad saw something in the dead of the night, when any decent being was tucked up in bed. Miss Alice wants us to see if there are any strangers on the estate."

Tony tried not to smile. But it was hard not to. He would be searching for himself.

The search party went out to hunt for a stranger in the grounds. And, of course, they found no one.

CHAPTER 11
Caught

The next night, Tony and Joe were just finishing their day's work when the car passed them and Miss Alice waved out of the window.

"It's late for Miss Alice to be going out," Tony said to Joe.

"I heard she's going to volunteer at the hospital," Joe said. "She's a good lass, Miss Alice."

Tony was surprised Alice would leave her brother after the recent events, but it gave him his chance. Tonight, there would be no sister running to the rescue, stopping Fortune from speaking out. Tony's haunting of Fortune was working, and he was ready to crumble. Miss Alice could not save her brother this time.

That night the wind moaned past the trees. There was no moon, and the darkness was eerie – a perfect night for a haunting. Tony stood by the French windows and looked inside the house. Fortune was sitting by the fire, staring into the flames.

Tony drummed his fingernails on the glass. It sounded like the branch of a tree tapping on the window, or the bony fingers of a skeleton. Fortune looked up in an instant. *What did he see*, Tony wondered. Tony's white face? The face of his dead brother?

Fortune stood up and shouted, "Leave me be!"

Tony pulled at the doors and was surprised as they swung open. Someone must have forgotten to lock them. The curtains were caught by the wind and seemed to come alive as Tony stepped into the room.

There was terror in Fortune's eyes. Tony knew what he must say. Not a shout but a menacing whisper. Again, Tony felt as if his brother was there beside him, murmuring in his ear. "Tell the truth," Tony said, the ghostly words floating from his mouth. Not Tony's voice at all, but the voice of his brother. "Tell the truth."

Fortune fell to the floor and screamed, "Oh please, leave me be." He beat the ground with his fist. "Please leave me be."

And again Tony said softly, "Tell the truth."

Now Fortune had to tell him what he needed to know, Tony thought. To explain that he'd been mistaken, that Charlie hadn't been running away. Fortune had to admit that he'd let a man die because he had been afraid to say he'd made a mistake. Tony needed to hear Fortune say that.

"Tell the truth," Tony said again.

Suddenly, from another corner of the room – from the spot where she had been hiding – flew Alice. She grabbed Tony by the arm and held it tight. She was small, but a lot stronger than she looked. "I knew it was you," Alice said. "It had to be. I knew if you thought I was gone you would try it again. I've been waiting! Why are you doing this to my brother?"

Tony struggled in Alice's grip. Now Fortune could see this was no ghost. This was a boy, made of flesh and blood. But the face ... Tony could see how puzzled Fortune looked, because the face was the same – the face that terrified him.

"Why are you doing this?" Miss Alice shouted again.

"Ask him!" Tony yelled. "Fortune knew my brother. My brother Charlie."

"I'd get the law on you!" Alice cried. "But you're not worth it. Get off our estate and don't come back. If I find you here again, I'll have you arrested."

Fortune began to laugh. "He wasn't a ghost, Alice." His voice was almost a giggle. Tony stopped struggling. Alice's grip loosened. "He wasn't a ghost." Fortune's laughter grew, becoming hysterical. He pulled himself onto a chair and rocked back and forth. "He wasn't a ghost," Fortune repeated. "He hadn't come back."

"Who hadn't come back?" Alice said, then turned to Tony. "What have you done to my brother?"

"It's what *he* did that matters," Tony said. "Tell him to confess. That's all I want."

"Confess to what?" Alice's eyes went from Tony to her brother. "Confess to what?!"

But Fortune wouldn't confess. Not now. Not now he knew it had all been a trick.

I'm sorry, Charlie, Tony thought. *I failed you again.*

In an instant, the temperature plunged. The room was suddenly icy cold. Tony's breath froze in the air. The curtains billowed at the windows. Fortune's gaze turned towards them and his eyes grew wide, his face shocked. Then Fortune looked back at Tony. "How are you doing that ... is this another trick?" Fortune demanded. A second later, he was staring again at the window. "No! Stay back," Fortune said.

Tony followed his horrified gaze. There was nothing at the windows. Tony knew then that he'd driven Fortune mad, and he felt a pang of guilt.

Fortune pulled himself to his feet. He looked again at Tony and said, "How are you doing this?" Then he yelled, "Tell me how you're doing this!"

CHAPTER 12

Back from the Grave

Fortune squeezed his fists so hard that Tony was sure his nails must be biting into his palms. He would see blood dripping through Fortune's fingers any moment.

"This is a trick. I will not stand for it." Fortune made his voice sound clear and unafraid. "I'm warning you!"

But who was Fortune talking to? Alice let out a gasp as Fortune lifted the poker by the fireplace and threw it. It crashed against the windows and sent shards of smashing glass everywhere. Alice threw Tony away from her and ran to her brother.

She tried to hold Fortune to her, but he struggled. "What is wrong?" Alice asked.

"The poker must have hit him," Fortune moaned. "It must have, so why didn't he cry out? Why didn't he fall?" Then his voice grew strong again as he said, "I am your commanding officer! Obey my orders and leave!" Fortune pushed Alice from him and she fell on the floor. He moved towards the windows. "I will beat you with my bare hands. I will bring you down." But Tony still didn't understand who Fortune was talking to. There was nobody there!

It was Tony's chance to escape, but he couldn't move. It was as if he was in a dream. He had to see how this would end.

Fortune stepped back, as if something was moving towards him. "Leave me be!" Fortune yelled. "I beg you. Leave me be!"

Alice was back on her feet. She put her arms around her brother. He clutched at her hand and said, "No, look, he's there." Fortune pointed to the windows. "You must see him. There."

Alice followed Fortune's gaze. It was a moment before she spoke. "There's no one there," she said softly.

Fortune began to shake. "No. No, he's there! He's coming closer. He won't stop. You must see him."

Alice shook her head and repeated, "There is no one there."

"He's dead, Alice," Fortune told her. "I know. I watched him die. He died in front of a firing squad in France."

Fortune closed his eyes and said, "Do you know what his last words were? 'I'll be back,' that's what he said. And he looked right at me as he said them. 'I will be back. And you will tell the truth.'"

Tears rolled down Fortune's face. "His last words, and they have haunted me ever since. I don't want to remember. I don't want to think of him. I just want to forget. But he won't let me." Fortune looked up again at something only he could see.

"Can't you hear him, Alice?" Fortune asked. "*Tell the truth*, it's what he always says. I can hear him from beyond the grave."

Fortune slumped against his sister. "I will only have peace if I confess."

CHAPTER 13

The Truth at Last

This was the moment. The moment when Tony would hear the truth.

Fortune was on the floor, his sister's arms around him. He was staring at nothing, but Tony knew what he was seeing. Fortune was looking into the past, and it terrified him.

Fortune's words came in soft whispers.

"That day, the rain was falling steadily in the cold dawn light. The platoon had moved up to the front line that the first wave had already gone over. We were the second wave.

I shouted out, 'Any moment now it'll be our turn, men.' I tried to sound in command, but I was so scared. We would never make it, I knew that. I was going to die. We were all going to die. Yet I tried to speak to my men as if I had no fear."

Fortune went on, "I watched my cold breath rising in the air. Bullets flew overhead. Flashes from the explosions lit up the clouds. Every bomb shook the ground like an earthquake. My hand was trembling. But it wasn't just the thought of death that I feared. In the short time I'd been there, I'd seen too many men go home missing limbs, crippled. They might have survived the trenches, but their lives would never be the same again. And every thought like this made me tremble more."

Fortune took a long deep breath.

"No more," Alice told him.

"I have to go on," Fortune said.

Yes, he has to go on, Tony thought.

It was a moment before he spoke again. "It was hell – a nightmare day. The stench of explosion fumes mixed with the fog. It got thicker and made everyone in the trench cough. We waited to be given the sign to go over the top. And I suddenly knew I couldn't do it. I stepped back. I turned and I ran. I heard the men calling after me. But I couldn't stop. I didn't care. There was so much smoke. I felt I was invisible. I was lost in the smoke. I could run and run and no one would ever find me.

"Bullets whizzed past my ears. Shells landed everywhere, throwing up giant geysers of mud. The whole place was churned up and full of shell holes.

"I slid into one of the holes. Covered my ears. I could hear shouts and screams and explosions, no matter how I tried to blot them out.

"I was going to wait till the firing died down, and then I would crawl away and hide. And then ... he came."

Fortune took a deep breath and closed his eyes, as if he had to force himself to go on.

"Who came?" Alice asked.

"It was him – that young soldier. He was heading back to the trench, carrying a big bag of ammunition. It was almost as big as he was. He looked at me as if he couldn't believe what he was seeing and said, 'What are you doing here, sir?' I couldn't even answer him. My teeth were shaking. 'Sir?' he asked. 'Sir!'

"I snatched up my pistol and pointed it at him. 'I'm not going back,' I said. 'I'm not going back.'

"'You've got to, sir.' He dared to say that to me! 'The men need you. Come on, I'll be with you.' He was offering to help. To help ME! He was ready to go back – he wasn't afraid. I hated him even more for that. He touched my arm, and I pulled away from him.

"'We've got to go, sir,' he said. I wanted to pull the trigger of that pistol so much, I don't know what stopped me. Then the moment was gone. I heard the horrible terrifying whistle of a shell, and it was coming straight for us. Then another, and another.

"'I've got to get this ammunition to the men, sir,' he said. And then he was gone, heading back to the trench. Running straight towards the explosions. Running back into the battle. I was alone. I threw myself to the dirt, just as a massive explosion ripped open the earth around me."

Finally, Tony had the truth. A truth he hadn't even expected. He murmured, "He wasn't running away. My brother wasn't running away."

Fortune went on as if he hadn't heard him. "More shells landed. The noise was deafening. There was nothing else to do but lie still and take it. And so I lay there, with my hands over my ears, praying that I wouldn't be hit. The shells moved on at last, creeping along the line to the left. And I knew it was over for me. The boy would go back and he would tell them where he'd found me. They had all seen me run off. They would know what I'd done. I almost turned the pistol on myself, but I was too much of a coward to even do that. I just sat where I was and waited."

CHAPTER 14

A Coward's Fate

Tony expected Fortune to stop, but still he went on. "It was much later – when the front was quiet – that I found out all of the men had been killed. Everyone who had seen me run off. All of them dead. Everyone apart from the boy. He could tell the world about my cowardice. But he was found unconscious, out of the trench. It looked as if he had been running away, and that was when I did the worst thing I have ever done. Before he could say a word against me, I spoke against him. I told my superiors he was the one who had deserted in the face of the enemy. I said I'd seen him running. That I'd tried to stop him. I had been wounded –

shrapnel in my shoulder. I said I'd been blown out by the blast. I looked like a hero."

Alice began to cry. "No. No. But why?"

"You think you can be brave, Alice, until you're faced with death," Fortune said. "I couldn't face death, and I couldn't face the shame of what I'd done."

Tony stepped forward. He was almost crying too. "My brother was shot because of you!"

Fortune was nodding. "He tried to tell everyone it was me who'd been running away, but no one listened. No one believed a private against an officer."

"But you let Charlie be executed," Tony said. "A firing squad. You let him have the shame of being a coward." Tony felt like leaping at Fortune and beating him with his fists. "You let him die."

Now Fortune was crying, his tears streaming down his face. "I know. I know. And I saw him die. I was ordered to go to his execution. I didn't want to. And I've never ever been able to forget that day."

Fortune seemed to go back again – to that place, that time that he only wanted to forget. "It was a bleak, dark day, and raining again," he said. "It always seemed to be raining – a steady, sad sort of rain. The parade ground was drab and grey. Your brother came out and didn't even look at me. He marched tall, his head up, as if he still wasn't afraid. It was me who was afraid, and I wasn't about to face a firing squad. I had not wanted to see it. Not like this. I'd wanted him to be dragged to his death, screaming. I wanted him to look like a coward." For the first time since he'd started his story, Fortune looked at Tony and added, "Your brother didn't do that. He went to his death like a soldier.

"I can still see it all, as if it's a moving picture. I see it every day. Can't get it out of my head." Fortune covered his face with his hands and sobbed. "The ground was scarred and dotted where previous bullets from the firing squad had hit. And then the military policeman led him to the wooden post, which backed onto a brick wall.

"The firing squad was made up of young privates hardly older than your brother. They were just soldiers like he was – like we all were. They were under orders to do a job.

"The military policeman offered him a cigarette. He shook his head.

"And when he was given the blindfold, he refused it. For me, that was the worst of all. I wanted him to wear that blindfold so I wouldn't have to see his eyes. Then he was alone, standing against the wooden post, staring ahead.

"The sergeant called the firing squad to attention. And at that moment, what I had been dreading happened. He turned and looked right at me."

Fortune sobbed again and struggled to speak. His next words came out in a mumbled cry, but Tony could understand every word. "I will never forget his eyes ... nor what he said. The words that have been haunting me since that day:

"'I will be back, and you will tell the truth.'"

Fortune grabbed Tony's arm. "Now I have. I've told the truth. Will he leave me be?"

CHAPTER 15

No Longer a Coward

It was another grey morning. Another parade of soldiers was returning from the war. Flags waved, bunting flew, people cheered them on. Small boys marched proudly beside the soldiers, carrying wooden sticks carved into guns. The soldiers looked broken, but the cheering crowds kept them going. Tony saw them holding themselves taller, steadying their pace. The cheering made them feel like heroes, and heroes they were, Tony thought. Every last one of them ...

Even the ones who didn't come back. Even the boys who had died at dawn.

And it might have been another grey morning, but for Tony the sun was shining.

The truth was out. Lieutenant Fortune had at last confessed, and Charlie's name had been cleared.

"So, is *Fortune* to be shot at dawn?" one of their neighbours had asked.

Tony had almost smiled. Shoot an officer? No, Fortune was now in a military hospital, too disturbed by his experiences to live a normal life. He would be there for a long time.

He'd been stripped of his medals, no longer a hero. His reputation was destroyed. Perhaps that was punishment enough for him.

Yet, in spite of what Fortune had done, Tony felt sorry for him. He hated thinking it, but he did. Fortune was really just a boy himself. Not much older than Charlie.

Perhaps the world would never know the whole story. Perhaps it didn't need to. The world knew Tony's big brother had not died a coward. In fact, the truth was that he'd died a hero.

"The boys look so good," his mother said as she clung on to Tony's arm and watched the soldiers. "Their mothers must be so proud of them."

"Their mothers deserve to be proud of them all, Ma, just like you are," Tony said.

His mother smiled when he said that, and nodded her head. Tony had lost his beloved brother, but at least now he had his ma back again. She stood taller and held her head high.

Now everyone knew the truth, and no one lowered their gaze when they passed them. Not now. Tony could look anyone in the eye.

"Such a terrible war," Ma said. "But at least there will never be another like it."

It had been the war to end all wars, people said. Tony watched the boys playing with their toy guns and hoped that was true.

The parade passed. The crowd began to thin out. And there on the other side of the street ...

... stood Charlie.

No, it couldn't be. Tony caught his breath. The figure in uniform stood silent, just watching. Tony glanced at Ma, but she was still smiling, waving her flag and watching the last of the soldiers as they marched away. Tony looked back. The figure smiled, and ... oh, it was Charlie's smile all right. Tony could never mistake that smile. The figure lifted his hand in a salute and then was gone, like mist, before Tony could even wave back.

Tony blinked. Had he imagined it? Had he really seen his brother?

And then he realised that it didn't matter. His brother would always be with him. The memory of him would last for ever. "Goodbye, Charlie," Tony whispered.

And he took out the white feather he had kept in his pocket, opened his palm and watched it float off into the sky.

Our books are tested
for children and young people by
children and young people.

Thanks to everyone who consulted on
a manuscript for their time and effort in
helping us to make our books better
for our readers.